THE JACKAL AND THE WAR DRUM.

GOMAYA THE JACKAL HAD NOT EATEN FOR MANY DAYS AND WAS VERY HUNGRY.

IF I DON'T FIND S[...] FOOD SOON, I'[...]

AS HE WANDERED THROUGH THE FOREST IN SEARCH OF FOOD HE CAME UPON AN OLD BATTLEFIELD.

WHAT'S THAT NOISE? I'D BETTER RUN BEFORE I'M ATTACKED.

WHIR WHOOSH

WHIR! WHOOSH!

ZOOM

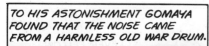

MORALS: FEAR OF THE UNKNOWN BRINGS NO GAIN.

THE COBRA AND THE CROW.

ONCE, THERE LIVED A PAIR OF CROWS ON AN OLD TREE. IN THE HOLLOW OF THE SAME TREE THERE LIVED A WICKED COBRA.

EVERY TIME I LAY EGGS, THIS WICKED COBRA EATS THEM ALL UP. WHAT SHALL WE DO?

LET'S ASK OUR FRIEND, THE JACKAL. HE'S A CLEVER FELLOW.

SAY FRIEND, THERE'S A BAD OLD COBRA WHO LIVES IN OUR TREE. HE EATS ALL OUR CHILDREN. HOW CAN WE GET RID OF HIM AND PROTECT OUR HOME?

J.JACKAL

THE JACKAL THOUGHT FOR A WHILE.

THEN —

I'LL TELL YOU HOW. LISTEN TO ME CAREFULLY. B..z..z..z....

ACCORDING TO PLAN, THE CROWS FLEW OVER A LAKE WHERE THE QUEEN AND HER MAIDS WERE BATHING. THEY HAD LEFT THEIR CLOTHES AND JEWELRY ON THE BANK OF THE LAKE.

NOW YOU KNOW WHAT TO DO.

THE FEMALE CROW SWOOPED DOWN, PICKED UP A GOLD NECKLACE AND FLEW OFF.

FLAP!

FLAP!

SOME OF THE KING'S SERVANTS, WHO WERE WORKING NEARBY, HEARD THE WOMEN SHOUTING . THEY BEGAN CHASING THE CROW.

SHE FLEW OVER THE HOME OF THE BAD COBRA AND DROPPED THE NECKLACE NEARBY.

A COBRA.

THE COBRA CAME OUT...

... AND THE ANGRY SERVANTS SAW HIM.

KILL HIM! KILL HIM!

BAM

THUD

THAT WAS THE END OF THE WICKED OLD COBRA.

THE MEN GOT BACK THE GOLD CHAIN AND THE CROWS LIVED HAPPILY EVER AFTER.

MORAL : MIGHTY BRAWN IS NO MATCH FOR NIMBLE BRAIN.

THE TURTLE WHO FELL OFF A STICK.

Near a certain lake there lived a turtle and two swans. They spent most of their time in telling each other stories.

AND SO IT CAME TO PASS...

So the years passed. Then suddenly one year there was a drought.

THE LAKE IS ALMOST DRY. HOW CAN WE LIVE WITHOUT WATER?

DON'T WORRY. WE WILL FIND A WAY OUT.

Suddenly the turtle had an idea.

FIRST FIND A LAKE FULL OF WATER. THEN BRING ME A STICK. I'LL HOLD ON TO THE MIDDLE OF IT. YOU HOLD THE ENDS AND CARRY ME TO OUR NEW LAKE.

GOOD, BUT WHILE WE ARE FLYING, TAKE CARE THAT YOU DON'T OPEN YOUR MOUTH.

MORAL : SILENCE IS GOLDEN.

THE MONKEY AND THE LOG.

ONE OF THEM PERCHED HIMSELF ON THE HALF-SAWN LOG.

WHAT IS THIS PIECE OF WOOD DOING HERE?

I WONDER WHAT WILL HAPPEN IF I PULL IT OUT?

SO HE PULLED AT THE WEDGE.

UGH! IT'S TOUGH.

OUT IT CAME.

HELP

THE GAP CLOSED IN, TRAPPING THE MONKEY'S LEG.

SNAP

THE POOR MONKEY WAS INSTANTLY KILLED.

MORAL : DO NOT MEDDLE WITH THINGS THAT DO NOT CONCERN YOU.

A MERCHANT AND A KING'S SERVANT.

GORAMBA THE KING'S SWEEPER CAME TO THE WEDDING, TOO, BUT UNINVITED.

DANTILA WAS FURIOUS.

GET OUT, GORAMBA! HOW DARE YOU COME HERE?

I'LL GET EVEN WITH HIM SOMEHOW.

THE WHOLE OF THAT NIGHT HE THOUGHT ABOUT IT.

AT LAST JUST BEFORE SUNRISE —

I'VE GOT IT!

THAT MORNING WHEN GORAMBA WENT TO SWEEP THE KING'S CHAMBER —

SHAME ON DANTILA! HOW DARE HE EMBRACE THE QUEEN!

THAT VERY EVENING DANTILA INVITED GORAMBA TO HIS HOME.

MY FRIEND, PLEASE ACCEPT THESE GIFTS AND FORGIVE ME FOR MY BEHAVIOUR THAT DAY.

THANK YOU SIR, THANK YOU.

I FORGIVE YOU. AND YOU WILL SEE AGAIN HOW CLEVER I CAN BE.

THE NEXT MORNING GORAMBA WAS SWEEPING THE KING'S ROOM AS USUAL.

HO! HO! HA! HA! OUR KING EATS CUCUMBERS IN THE LAVATORY.

MORAL : EVERY DOG HAS ITS DAY.

THE MERCHANT'S SON AND THE IRON BALANCE.

THEN SUDDENLY HE HAD AN IDEA.

SURE. WHY NOT!

WELL! FRIEND. I CAN'T BLAME YOU. ANYWAY I'LL GO FOR A BATH. CAN YOU SEND YOUR LITTLE SON WITH ME TO HELP ME CARRY MY BELONGINGS?

SO THE LITTLE BOY ACCOMPANIED JWEERNADHANA AND CARRIED HIS BELONGINGS FOR HIM.

ON THE WAY THEY CAME UPON A CAVE.

LET'S ENTER IT AND SEE WHAT IT'S LIKE INSIDE.

ONCE INSIDE, JWEERNADHANA LEFT THE BOY AND QUICKLY RAN OUT.

THEN HE BLOCKED THE ENTRANCE WITH A HUGE BOULDER.

WELL! NOW THE BOY CAN'T COME OUT.

THEN HE RETURNED TO HIS FRIEND.

WHY ARE YOU ALONE? WHERE IS MY LITTLE SON?

I'M SORRY, FRIEND. A FLAMINGO PICKED HIM UP AND FLEW OFF.

WHAT! YOU LIAR! HOW COULD THAT BE? BRING BACK MY SON OR I'LL TAKE YOU TO THE JUDGE.

LET'S GO. I'M NOT AFRAID!

SO THEY WENT TO THE JUDGE.

JUDGE, THIS ROGUE HAS KIDNAPPED MY ONLY SON. I WANT JUSTICE.

JWEERNADHANA, I COMMAND YOU TO RETURN HIS SON TO HIM.

MORAL : **TIT FOR TAT.**

THE JACKAL WHO FELL INTO A VAT OF INDIGO DYE.

ONCE A JACKAL GOT SO HUNGRY THAT HE VENTURED INTO A TOWN IN SEARCH OF FOOD.

TO SAVE HIMSELF FROM THE DOGS HE RAN INTO A DYER'S YARD AND...

...FELL INTO A VAT OF INDIGO DYE.

WHEN HE CAME OUT THE DOGS COULD NOT RECOGNISE HIM. THEY RAN AWAY IN PANIC.

BACK IN THE JUNGLE THE OTHER ANIMALS TOO WERE FRIGHTENED.

THUS ASSURED, THE ANIMALS RETURNED. THEN —

CHASE ALL THESE DIRTY JACKALS AWAY. I SHALL HAVE NOTHING TO DO WITH THEM.

THAT NIGHT WHEN THE JUNGLE WAS ABSOLUTELY STILL, THE JACKALS BEGAN HOWLING.

WOOOOOOOO WOOOOOOOO

TRUE TO HIS NATURE THE BLUE JACKAL BEGAN HOWLING ALONG WITH HIS BROTHERS.

HEY! OUR KING IS ONLY A JACKAL. WE HAVE BEEN FOOLED. HE SHALL DIE FOR THIS.

WOOOOOOO

SO THEY POUNCED ON THE BLUE JACKAL AND...

...THAT WAS THE END OF HIM.

MORAL : A COAT OF PAINT CANNOT HIDE ONE'S TRUE COLOURS.

THE HERON AND THE CRAB.

AN OLD HERON LIVED IN A JUNGLE NEAR A BIG LAKE WHICH WAS FULL OF FISHES, CRABS AND OTHER WATER CREATURES.

I AM SO OLD AND FEEBLE, I CAN HARDLY CATCH ANY FISH. UNLESS I FIND A WAY OUT, I WILL SOON DIE.

ONE DAY HE SAT AT THE EDGE OF THE LAKE AND BEGAN CRYING. A CRAB CAME TO HIM.

UNCLE, WHAT'S THE MATTER? WHY ARE YOU CRYING? AREN'T YOU GOING TO EAT ANY FISH TODAY?

FROM TODAY I SHALL FAST UNTO DEATH.

BUT WHY?

AN ASTROLOGER TOLD ME THIS MORNING THAT THERE WILL BE NO RAIN FOR 12 YEARS. THE LAKES WILL DRY UP. WE SHALL ALL DIE.

THE CRAB TOLD THIS TO ALL THE OTHER WATER CREATURES. THEY WERE PANIC-STRICKEN.

THEY SENT THE CRAB TO ASK THE HERON WHAT THEY SHOULD DO.

THIS MEANS SURE DEATH FOR US. PLEASE TELL US HOW WE CAN SAVE OURSELVES.

WELL, NOT FAR AWAY THERE IS A BIG LAKE, WHICH WILL NEVER DRY UP. I WILL TAKE YOU THERE, ONE BY ONE.

THE HERON HAD SUCCEEDED IN GAINING THEIR CONFIDENCE.

UNCLE! BROTHER!
FATHER ME FIRST!
NO ME!
PLEASE!

THE WICKED HERON TOOK THEM, ONE BY ONE, TO A ROCK NEARBY AND ATE THEM.

THE MINUTE, THE HERON SAID THIS, THE CRAB CAUGHT HIS NECK BETWEEN HIS CLAWS AND STRANGLED HIM.

THAT WAS THE END OF THE WICKED OLD HERON.

THE CRAB GRIPPED THE HERON BY HIS NECK AND DRAGGED HIM SLOWLY TO THE LAKE.

HA! HA! HA! FASTING TO DEATH! POOR FISHES.

WHEN HE REACHED THE LAKE HE WAS STILL LAUGHING.

CRAB, WHY ARE YOU BACK? WHAT HAS HAPPENED TO UNCLE? WE ARE ALL WAITING FOR OUR TURN, TO BE TAKEN TO THE OTHER POND.

YOU FOOLS, HE HAS EATEN ALL YOUR BROTHERS. I FOUND OUT AND KILLED HIM.

MORAL: ONE MAY SMILE AND SMILE AND YET BE A VILLAIN.

DHARMABUDDHI AND PAPABUDDHI.

IN A CERTAIN VILLAGE THERE ONCE LIVED TWO FRIENDS CALLED. DHARMABUDDHI AND PAPABUDDHI. PAPABUDDHI WAS A DISHONEST MAN.

IF I CAN GET DHARMABUDDHI TO START SOME BUSINESS WITH ME, I CAN CHEAT HIM OF HIS SHARE AND BECOME A RICH MAN.

SO HE WENT TO DHARMABUDDHI.

FRIEND, I HAVE AN IDEA. LET US GO OUT INTO THE WORLD AND MAKE SOME MONEY.

WHY NOT?

SO THEY SET OFF TOWARDS THE NEAREST TOWN.

THEY SOON MADE A LOT OF MONEY AND WERE ON THEIR WAY BACK HOME. SUDDENLY PAPABUDDHI ASKED HIS FRIEND TO HALT.

A THOUGHT JUST STRUCK ME. IT IS NOT SAFE TO TAKE ALL THE MONEY BACK WITH US. LET US TAKE ONLY A SMALL SUM AND BURY THE REST HERE.

QUITE RIGHT. LET'S.

THE NEXT DAY PAPABUDDHI WENT TO DHARMABUDDHI'S HOUSE.

SO OFF THEY WENT. BUT WHEN THEY DUG UP THE PIT, THE POT OF MONEY WAS NOWHERE TO BE SEEN.

QUARRELLING ALL THE WAY, THEY WENT TO THE JUDGE.

I DIDN'T.

YOU DID.

THIS MAN HAS STOLEN THE MONEY. THE FOREST GOD IS MY WITNESS. HE WILL SPEAK THE TRUTH.

ALL RIGHT. WE WILL GO TO THE FOREST TOMORROW.

PAPABUDDHI WENT STRAIGHT HOME TO HIS FATHER.

FATHER, I HAVE STOLEN DHARMABUDDHI'S MONEY. YOU WILL HAVE TO DO AS I SAY IF I AM TO ESCAPE.

I'LL DO AS YOU WANT ME TO, MY SON.

THE NEXT MORNING DHARMABUDDHI, PAPABUDDHI, THE JUDGE AND THE VILLAGE ELDERS WENT UP TO WHERE THE MONEY HAD BEEN BURIED.

O TREE GOD. TELL US WHO THE THIEF IS!

DHARMABUDDHI IS THE THIEF.

WHILE THE OTHERS WERE BUSY DISCUSSING THE CASE, DHARMABUDDHI WAS BUSY COLLECTING DRIED LEAVES AND TWIGS. THESE HE PLACED NEAR THE HOLLOW OF THE TREE AND ---

... SET THEM ALIGHT.

AS THE FIRE ROSE INTO THE HOLLOW, OUT RAN PAPABUDDHI'S FATHER.

THE JUDGE UNDERSTOOD ALL AND WAS ANGRY.

FOR THIS CRIME HE SHALL BE HANGED ON THIS VERY TREE RIGHT NOW.

MORAL: HONESTY IS THE BEST POLICY.

THE LION AND THE HARE.

IN A CERTAIN JUNGLE THERE LIVED A LION CALLED BHASURAKA. HE WAS VERY STRONG AND KILLED THE ANIMALS IN THE JUNGLE JUST FOR FUN.

GRRRR

OH! WHY DOES HE HAVE TO KILL US WHEN HE IS NOT HUNGRY?

ONE DAY ALL THE SURVIVING ANIMALS APPROACHED BHASURAKA.

MASTER, WHY KILL US ALL WHEN ONE OF US WOULD SATISFY YOUR HUNGER? FROM TODAY ONE OF US WILL COME TO YOU EACH DAY. IN RETURN YOU MUST LET THE OTHERS LIVE IN PEACE.

ALL RIGHT. BUT IF YOU FAIL TO COME, I SHALL KILL ALL OF YOU.

EVERY DAY THE ANIMALS DREW LOTS. ONE DAY —

OH! POOR HARE! IT IS YOUR TURN TODAY.

MOST RELUCTANTLY THE HARE MADE HIS WAY TO BHASURAKA.

I WISH I COULD KILL HIM AND SAVE MY LIFE!

SUDDENLY HE CAME ACROSS A WELL. HE WAS JUBILANT.

NOW I KNOW A WAY TO KILL HIM. AND I WON'T FAIL.

BY THE TIME THE HARE REACHED BHASURAKA IT WAS SUNSET. AND BHASU-RAKA WAS FURIOUS.

THE FIRST THING I'LL DO TOMOR-ROW IS TO KILL ALL THE ANIMALS.

CAUTIOUSLY THE HARE NEARED BHASURAKA.

AS IT IS YOU ARE SMALL. APART FROM THAT, YOU ARE LATE. I'LL KILL YOU NOW AND THE OTHERS TOMORROW.

MORAL : NOTHING IS IMPOSSIBLE FOR A CLEVER MAN.